GHOST in the HOUSE

17

Written by Elizabeth Bolton
Illustrated by Ray Burns

Troll Associates

Library of Congress Cataloging in Publication Data

Bolton, Elizabeth.
    Ghost in the house.

    Summary: When Peter gets blamed for losing all the
things that have been disappearing around his house, he
starts looking for the real thief.
    1. Children's stories, American. [1. Lost and found
possessions—Fiction. 2. Mystery and detective stories]
I. Burns, Raymond, 1924-   ill. II. Title.
PZ7.B63597Gh   1985   [Fic]   84-20530
ISBN 0-8167-0418-X (lib. bdg.)
ISBN 0-8167-0419-8 (pbk.)

GHOST in the HOUSE

Peter was quiet at breakfast Friday morning. He was worried, but nobody noticed.

Mom was making pancakes. She was trying not to step on Wags. Wags was still a puppy and he often got in the way.

Peter's big sister Susan was thinking about going skating with her friends that night.

Peter's big brother, Bobby, was thinking
about the deep snow that had just fallen.
Bobby wanted to stay home from school and
play in it.

Peter loved to play in the snow, too.
But that wasn't what he was thinking about.
He was worrying about his new red scarf.
Aunt Kate had given it to him for Christmas.
But Peter didn't know where it was.

"You're careless, Peter Wilson!" That's what his mother would say if he told her.

I *used* to lose things all the time, he thought. That's when I was little. But I'm bigger now. I *am* careful.

Nobody else thought so though. Whenever things got lost, people said, "It must be Peter's fault. He's so careless."

Mom put a plate of pancakes on the kitchen table. "Call your father," she said to Susan. Just then Dad came in. He was frowning.

"Has anybody seen my silver pen?" he asked.

"It was in your jacket pocket last night," Susan said. "Remember? You signed my report card after dinner."

"It's not there now," Dad said. "Somebody must have borrowed it."

Everybody looked at each other.

"I didn't," Mother said. "I have my own pen."

"I didn't," Susan said. "I did my homework at the library."

"I didn't," Bobby said. "I used a pencil for my homework."

Dad sat down and drank his orange juice. "My pen didn't walk away by itself. Somebody must have borrowed it."

"It was probably Peter," Bobby said in
a grown-up voice. "He probably lost it.
He loses everything. You lost your new scarf,
didn't you, Pete? I wanted to use it when I
walked Wags this morning. But it wasn't on
your hook."

"I *didn't* lose it!" Peter's voice was like a croak. "I *know* I wasn't careless! And I didn't take Dad's pen!"

Susan shook her head. "A lot of things get lost around here!" she said. "I can't find my striped skating cap. I know I had it two nights ago! And Bobby can't find his ruler. *Somebody* is taking them!"

"Maybe we have a ghost in the house!"
Bobby made his voice sound scary.

"I don't think we have a ghost," Dad
said. "I think we have *carelessness*."

He didn't look at Peter. He didn't have
to. Peter knew just what Dad was thinking.

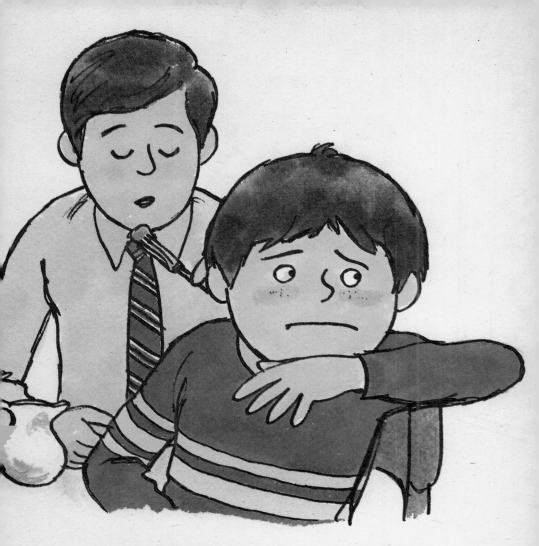

I'm *not* careless anymore, Peter thought. I
know I didn't lose those things!

Bobby was right. It was just as if they
had a ghost in the house. I have to find the
ghost, Peter thought. Otherwise nobody will
believe I wasn't careless!

Peter didn't pay attention in school that
day. He didn't hear the teacher call on him.
He was trying to figure out how to catch
their ghost. Outside the classroom windows,
the sky turned gray. Snowflakes were falling
thick and fast when school was over.

Peter put on his mittens and boots. He didn't throw snowballs with the other boys. He and Bobby walked home from the bus stop without talking. The icy snowflakes stung their faces.

Home was warm and cozy. The air smelled of chocolate. "I bet Mom made brownies!" Bobby said. Peter didn't answer. He put his mittens in his coat pocket. He hung his coat on its hook. Wags sniffed it. He was always nosy. Peter pushed him away.

Mom had brownies and hot cocoa waiting. "Have you seen my big red pot holder?" she asked. "I can't find it anywhere."

"We know Peter didn't lose that," Bobby joked. "Peter can't cook." He poked Peter in the ribs. But Peter didn't grin back. Now there was something else to find.

Wags came into the kitchen. His leash was in his mouth and he was wiggling all over. Mom laughed. "Take him out, will you, Peter? He wants to play in the snow. He's been waiting all day."

I'll start looking for the ghost when I get back, Peter promised himself.

He put his boots back on. He put on his coat and his old scarf. He put his hands in his pockets for his mittens.

The mittens weren't there!

I wore them home! I had them on when I walked into the house! I didn't lose them, Peter thought.

He felt like crying. But he didn't let his mother or Bobby see. He hooked Wags' leash to his collar and went outside.

The snow was deep now. It was deeper
than Wags was tall. Wags loved jumping up
and landing *splat* in the snow. That was how
he ran—*jump*—*splat*.

Peter threw a snowball. Wags brought it
back. Peter made another snowball. That one
Wags ate. He sat down and barked and
waited for Peter to throw another.

The snowballs made Peter's fingers cold.
He threw a stick instead. Wags went after it.
Peter saw Wags' tail like a golden flag above
the snowdrift. *Zig, zag,* it went. But it didn't
come back again. Instead snow flew through
the air. Wags was burying the stick.

"Time to go in," Peter told Wags at last.
"I have some detective work to do."

They went back inside. Wags shook himself dry. Peter put his coat and boots away. Then he looked through the house from top to bottom. He looked for all the things that had gotten lost.

He looked behind the towels and sheets on closet shelves. He looked behind Dad's camera and in Mom's knitting bag. He looked in all the boxes and cartons in the cellar. Bobby and two friends were playing a game on the cellar floor. "What are you looking for?" they asked. Peter didn't tell them.

He looked under the bed in Mom and Dad's room. Nothing was there except the flowered rug. He looked all through the room he shared with Bobby. He looked in Susan's room, until she chased him out. Peter went back downstairs.

"Are you looking for Dad's pen?" asked Mom. "I already did. I looked everywhere but behind the couch. It's too heavy to move."

The pen couldn't fall down there, Peter knew. The couch was right up against the wall.

At dinner time Peter had to give up looking. He hadn't found his scarf or Dad's pen—or anything else that was missing.

Tomorrow, Peter thought, I'll sweep the snow off the front steps and the back porch. Maybe I *did* drop my scarf and mittens out there somewhere.

By morning the snow was too deep to sweep. More snow was falling. Soon it turned to sleet.

"No sledding till the sleet stops," Dad said firmly. "You boys can watch TV instead."

Bobby ran to turn on the TV. Only there weren't any cars or heroes on the screen. There were only wiggly lines and something that looked like snow.

Bobby groaned. Dad groaned, too. "The storm may have broken our antenna. Or maybe the trouble's easier to fix. We'll call Mr. Sands and see."

Soon Mr. Sands' repair truck came *toot-tooting* through the snow. Peter liked Mr. Sands. Mr. Sands never said, "Don't bother me, I'm busy." Sometimes he even let Peter help.

Maybe Mr. Sands could help me catch our ghost, Peter thought. But first they had to fix the TV.

Wags came in to help. Peter pushed him
away. "Not now, Wags. I'm busy!"

"I'm sure glad to have you help me, Peter," Mr. Sands said. "Hand me the big screwdriver, please."

Peter looked. "There isn't any screwdriver here," he said.

"I just had it," said Mr. Sands. He looked
puzzled. "Give me the short-handled one
then, will you?" Peter handed it to him.
Then Peter went to find an old rag to let Mr.
Sands wipe off the parts inside the set.

"Keep the rag here, partner. I may have to do more dusting," Mr. Sands said. "Now I need the short screwdriver again."

Peter reached for it. His hands felt the
soft carpet—nothing more. Peter looked.
He looked again. "It's not here, Mr. Sands,"
he said.

"Now, it must be," Mr. Sands said
patiently. "I just gave it to you. You didn't go
anywhere." He crawled out from behind the
TV set. He looked at the floor. He looked in
his toolbox. His eyebrows rose.

"Peter," he said finally, "I've never believed in ghosts. I think now I do."

Dad came into the room. "Is something
else missing?"

Mr. Sands told Dad what had just
happened.

Dad and Peter told Mr. Sands about all
the things that were lost. Mr. Sands shook
his head. "Sure is a mystery!" he said.
"Hope I don't lose anything more." Dad
lent Mr. Sands a screwdriver so he could
finish his work.

"The TV is fine now," Mr. Sands said at last. "Here's your screwdriver. Put it away fast before it disappears! Peter, give me that rag. I want to dust everything again before I close this up."

The dust rag wasn't there!

"Nobody but the three of us have been in this room," Dad said slowly. "None of us have left."

"Except Wags," Peter said. "He was here. But I chased him off." He stopped suddenly and looked at the couch.

It stood against the wall as it always did.
But something was there where the couch
met the floor. Something fluffy. It *might*
have been a bit of dust. Only it looked like
something else Peter recognized.

Dad and Mr. Sands looked, too. Dad laughed, then put his finger to his lips. Tiptoe across the carpet went Peter. As quietly as possible, Peter took hold of the golden fluff.

Something under the couch let out a yelp!
It was Wags!

The little dog came wriggling out. Now Dad and Mr. Sands started to laugh. Mom came running in, and so did Bobby. Susan ran downstairs.

"I think Peter's solved our mystery," Dad said. He took hold of one side of the couch. Mr. Sands took hold of the other side. They moved the couch out from the wall.

There was Peter's scarf...and mittens...
and Susan's cap. There was Dad's pen and
Mother's pot holder and Bobby's ruler—and
Mr. Sands' tools. And a lot of other things
they hadn't even missed!

"Wags hid them to play with later," Peter
said, "just like he buried the stick outside in
the snow!"

"And we never saw him!" said Mr. Sands,
scratching Wags' head. "We never heard a
sound. He was just like a little ghost."

"I told you we had a ghost!" Bobby
crowed.

"It was a thief," laughed Peter. "Only it
was a four-legged one!"

The whole family went to the kitchen to have brownies and milk in honor of Peter's fine detective work. Mr. Sands joined them. And no one ever called Peter careless again.